NO
KISS FOR MOTHER

BY TOMI UNGERER

DELACORTE PRESS

NEW YORK

The text of this book has been reset in sixteen-point ITC Clearface, a contemporary adaptation of the typeface designed by Morris Fuller Benton in 1907.
The illustrations are pencil drawings.
Typography by Lynn Braswell.

Published by
Delacorte Press
Bantam Doubleday Dell Publishing Group, Inc.
666 Fifth Avenue
New York, New York 10103

Library of Congress Cataloging in Publication Data

Ungerer, Tomi, 1931–
No kiss for mother/by Tomi Ungerer.
      p.   cm.
Summary: Piper Paw cannot bear being kissed by his mother all the time, and it takes some painful experiences for them to reach a mutual understanding.
ISBN 0-385-30384-X (tr ed).—ISBN 0-385-30385-8 (lib bdg) [1. Mothers and sons—Fiction.   2. Cats—Fiction.]   I. Title.
PZ7.U43No   1991
[Fic]—dc20   90-44882   CIP   AC

Manufactured in the United States of America

May 1991

10   9   8   7   6   5   4   3   2   1

CHAPTER ONE

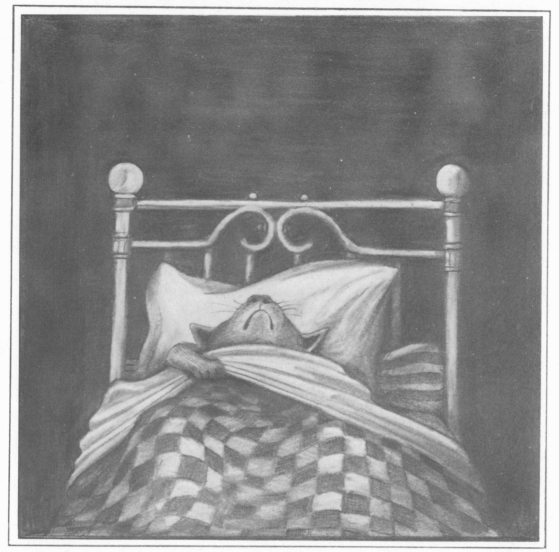

It is early in the morning.
In his warm and cozy bed,
sunk in a soundproof slumber,
Piper Paw dreams
of chasing mice in a pastry shop.

His alarm clock has not gone off,
because late last night, Piper took it apart.
He wanted to find out what seconds,
minutes, and hours looked like.
"That clock is full of them," he thought.
"I can hear them ticking and tacking.
I must see how they do it."
So he grabbed his flashlight, sneaked into the kitchen,
and fetched his mother's can opener.
With the opener he cut along the clock's rim
and pried it open with a fork.
The spring shot out with a snap
and coiled itself around the curious kitten's nose.

4

In a rage, Piper dumped the lifeless shell of
the clock out of the window,
along with the flashlight and can opener.
The missiles crashed seven floors below.
"That will teach it," he grumbled.

And now it is morning and time to wake up.
But Piper's mother, Mrs. Velvet Paw,
needs no alarm clock.
She gets up every day at the same time,
except on Sunday mornings, when they all brunch in bed.
"My, my, that Piper is still asleep," she says.
"He'll be late for breakfast.
I'd better go and wake my sweet little nestling up."
So she tippy-toes into her son's room.
"Time to get up," says Mother Paw.
Piper does not hear.
In his dream he has just cornered a purple mouse
between two wedding cakes.
"Time to get up, Honey Pie," calls Mother Paw
as she bends down to wedge a kiss in Sonny's ear.

And THAT wakes Piper up.
Piper hates to be kissed,
and to be kissed out of such a captivating dream
is just about the most annoying thing in the world.
With a hiss and a screech he jumps out of bed
and shoots off, growling, to the bathroom.

Piper does not wash because he does not like to.
He does not like to brush his teeth either.
When he reaches the bathroom,
he promptly latches the door to keep his mother out.
He turns on the water, lets it run, and wets his washcloth.
Then he rubs his toothbrush on the edge of the sink.
"In case Mother Snoop is listening," Piper says.
Then he takes it easy for a while,
looking at some soggy comic books
which he keeps behind the tub.

Meanwhile, in Piper's room,
Mother Paw has neatly laid out his clothing,
cleaned and pressed the night before.
Piper does not like that either.
He would rather choose his own outfit.
"I look like a mail-order dummy," Piper complains,
"neat and cute and tidy like a good little postcard pussy."
And every morning, with renewed rage,
he crumples and rumples his clothes
behind his mother's back.

"Breakfast is ready, darling," calls a motherly voice
for the eighth or ninth time.
Father Paw is already seated, and that can mean trouble.
"Come and sit down, my darling sweet," says Mrs. Paw.
"Have some of this mice mush, my darling.
Here, have some herring scraps and fried finch gizzards.
I made them especially for you, my darling."
"Don't you *darling* me, Mother.
It kills my appetite," snaps Piper.
"I am no Honey Pie either.
They'd throw me off the ball team if I played like a darling
or looked like a Honey Pie, and, furthermore,
you should be informed, sweet Mother Pie,
that there is no such thing as a Honey Pie.
I checked with Mr. Marzipan, the baker,
who is an authority on confections,
and he confirmed my suspicions.
There is no such thing as a Honey Pie."

"You just enjoy hurting my feelings,"
Mother Paw says between sniffles.
"Someday, when I am gone for good,
you will miss my little dishes.
Who knows?
You'll end up alone in this world
with no one to hug and love you,
no one to prepare your meals and clean up your mess."
"That will suit me just fine," snickers Piper.
"I am no baby,
and I'll gladly do without any gooey attentions."
Mother Paw is on the verge of tears.
"Stop talking to me that way," she moans.
"Each word is a nail in my coffin.
When I think of all the poor kittens in this world,
starving, freezing in forsaken back alleys,
my heart wrinkles with sorrow."

Father Paw does not say much.
Most of the time he does not talk at all,
especially at mealtime
when he'd rather chew on food than words.
"Enough is enough, and cut the nonsense," he orders Piper.
"Not another word from you.
There is such a thing as spanking,
and you should know it, Mister Smart.
If you have any doubts you can check it with my cane,
who is an authority on corrections."

There is silence around the breakfast table now.
Piper, his ears flattened, hides his muzzle in his bowl.
"Time to go," says Mr. Paw,
who works as supervisor in a rat-processing plant.

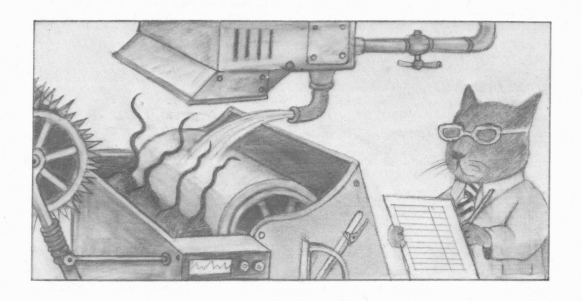

"Skip the bus, Piper.
I'll drive you to school today."
Father and son get up and slip on their overcoats.
Mother kisses her boy good-bye.
He makes a face and wipes off his jowls.
"Are you not going to kiss your mother good-bye?"
asks his father.
"No, not unless it's an emergency," replies Piper.

They take the elevator and emerge in the street.
At the sight of his car, Mr. Paw's eyes turn red with rage.
The windshield is cracked!
"My car, my only car," he gasps.
"Look at what the lousy punks have done to it.
Look at that!" he goes on,
pointing to an object lying in the gutter.
"They tried to break into the car with a can opener."

Piper says nothing as he climbs into the car.
He has not done his homework.
He can't even skip school,
now that his father is driving him there.
"What is all this fussing with your mother lately?"
asks Father Paw after a few blocks.
"She treats me like an infant," says Piper.
"She embarrasses me and drives me up the wall,
out of my blooming mind.
She'd have me wear diapers if she could."
"Some mothers are made that way," explains Father Paw.
"They can't help it. My mother was that way.
So was my father's mother.
Still, you should be nice to her. By the way,
any time you want me to build some bookshelves
in the bathroom, let me know.
No sense letting your literature mildew under the tub.
When I was your age I acted just like you.
Never brushed my teeth. Ha ha!
I fooled everyone by rubbing my toothbrush
on the edge of the sink.
Fooled everyone but the dentist.
You can still hear the echo in my cavities.
Well, here we are, son.
Don't kiss me. Have a good day."

16

Piper steps out and waves good-bye to his father.
There is no fooling the old cat.
Besides,
Piper really feels bad about the windshield.

CHAPTER TWO

In school, Piper is known as a rowdy.
He is the troublemaker of his class.
He is very ingenious when it comes to practical jokes.
He sprinkles itching powder or catnip on everyone,
stuffs the teacher's handbag with live spiders
(big black ones),
and pours airplane glue down the girls' necks.
His locker is an arsenal of contraband firecrackers,
noisemakers, smoke bombs, booby traps, peashooters—
in short, anything that comes in handy to disrupt his class.

Yet his grades are good,
for Piper has been blessed with an active brain.
When Piper has not bothered with his homework
(which is most of the time),
he usually manages to get himself
kicked out of class before homework inspection.
"It's better to have bad grades in conduct than in work,"
he tells the other pupils.
For today, Piper had planned to let off a stink bomb.
But the conversation with his father
and the cracked windshield have sobered him down.
So meek, so well behaved is he
that his teacher, Miss Purrypot, asks,
"Is anything ailing our jester?
Piper, you may be excused
to see the nurse if you find it necessary."
But Piper listlessly shakes his head.

At recess Piper's friends gang around him.

"You all right?"

"You sick or something?"

"What's up? Tell us," they all ask.

"I've got a hangover from too much kissing," he admits.

"Kissing?"

"Who is she?"

"You must be kidding."

"Is it Looloobah?"

"Is it Mitzy Bodyheat?"

"Or Miss Purrypot?"

And that brings down a gale of laughter.

"Who knows?" adds Jefferson, the bully of the class.

"It might have been the principal."

Piper can bear no more.

He hits Jefferson in the left eye

and catches him with an uppercut under the chin.

In a split and a slit of a second,
both cats are rolling on the ground,
hissing, hitting, biting and clawing,
to the delight of the young spectators,
who are taking sides and making bets.
"Go on, Jeffy, kiss him one."
"Sock him, Piper, below the belt."
It is a rainy day,
and both fighters turn into one ball of mud.
By the time recess is over,
the two cats are hardly recognizable.
Jefferson's left eye is swollen shut
and Piper's left ear is half torn off.
He is bleeding like a fountain.

"It seems our head clown has one ear left
to listen to my advice, which is:
Go to the infirmary at once," exclaims Miss Purrypot
as she sights the bleeding warriors.
"And you, Jefferson, will escort him there."
The two boys leave without a word.
"You look a mess.
Have a cigar—you'll need it," says Jefferson
as he pulls out a cigar butt and a lighter.
"It's a corona, fresh.
I picked it up in front of the opera house last night."
The boys, friends again,
disappear in the bathroom
to gather courage in a cloud of smoke.

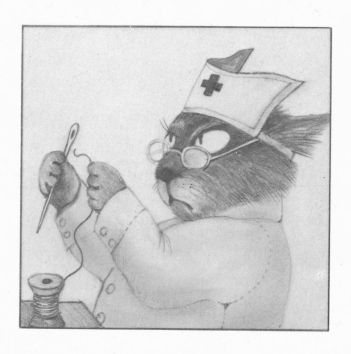

The trip to the infirmary turns out to be a punishment of its own.
Piper's ear has to be stitched back into place.
The nurse, Miss Clot,
does not have what is called a gentle touch (like Mother's).
She prefers iodine to Mercurochrome,
and that, holy mackerel, really, really hurts.
"I know your kind, you scoundrel," says the nurse
as she threads the biggest needle she can find.
"I know it was you who put a garter snake
in my medicine cabinet, you worthless imp.
Next time, I shall have the pleasure of clipping
your ear altogether."

Yowls of pain drown her words.
When the stitching is over,
Miss Clot wraps up Piper's head in a huge bandage.
"Well, Piper, with a red ribbon and a twig of holly
you'd look like a regular Christmas present,"
snickers the nurse as the two boys walk away.

"I say that Clot woman is downright vicious,"
says Jefferson compassionately.
"You should tell your mother about it."
"My mother!" says Piper.
"She would make such a fuss, you have no idea.
That would be even worse than all the pains in the world.
I just hope nobody heard me cry."

CHAPTER THREE

Today is Mrs. Velvet Paw's shopping day.
"I shall pick up my son at school and take him out for lunch,"
thinks Mrs. Paw as she gets ready.
"There is casserole of mole innards
on the menu at Zeldina's today,
my sweet Piper's favorite dish."

Mrs. Paw loves to take her son out and show him off.
Zeldina's restaurant is the best in town,
and there Piper gets all the attention and helpings
that befit Mother's young prince.
Velvet Paw and Zeldina are good friends.
They play canasta on Wednesday nights
and belong to the same bingo and bowling club.
Now it is noon.
Mrs. Paw eagerly waits for her son to come out.
She wears her cerise dress with matching hat and bag.
Cerise is Piper's favorite color.
The bell is ringing,
and the school disgorges its flow of screaming pupils.
Mrs. Paw searches for her son in the living rush.
A bandaged head emerges.

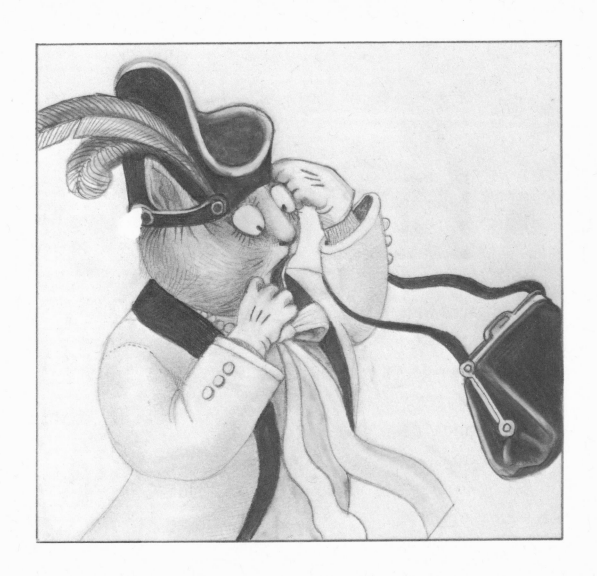

"Piper! My son, my Piper!"
she cries.

The sight of her wounded son
has left Mrs. Paw breathless.
Shaking,
blind with tears,
she snatches him out of the crowd
and carries him off in a torrent of kisses.
"My little sugar tiger,
what have they done to you?
Quick, a doctor!
To the hospital," she cries.
"Taxi, here, taxi."

Piper is mortified.
He yanks himself free, screaming:
"Don't kiss me in front of people.
Kisses, kisses all the time.
I don't like it. I don't want it.
GOOD-MORNING KISSES,
GOOD-EVENING KISSES,
THANK-YOU KISSES,
KISS-ME KISSES,
SORRY-DARLING KISSES,
SUMMER KISSES,
WINTER KISSES,
LICKY KISSES,
SLOPPY KISSES
SOGGY KISSES."
And Piper goes on
right there on the sidewalk.

Mother Paw does not know what to say, what to do.
For once she wishes she were a mouse
to crawl into the nearest crevice and hide.
The taxi Mrs. Paw has hailed is waiting at the curb.
"That's no way to talk to your mother," says the driver.
"You should be ashamed of yourself."
"Yes, that's right!" Mrs. Paw exclaims.
In an explosion of sudden anger,
she steps forward
and *slam-whack* she slaps her son into silence.
She orders Piper into the taxi
and gives the driver Zeldina's address.
Piper has never been hit by his mother before.
Glum mother, sullen son drive away.

The lunch at Zeldina's seems endless and tasteless.
Both are sorry for what has happened.
Neither can find any words.
There is nothing they can say.
Piper hardly touches his casserole of mole innards.
Mrs. Paw orders only a cup of tea.
When it is time to return to school,
Piper gets up and goes out of the restaurant
without taking leave.

At school, no one mentions the events.
But for his aching ear, it seems nothing has happened.
At afternoon recess, Piper goes to his locker
and brings out two stink bombs,
a high-velocity slingshot,
and an assortment of firecrackers.
Then he calls his pals over and says,
"I need money. It's all for sale."
The transaction takes place quickly.
Firecrackers are hard to come by,
and no one can manufacture stink bombs like Piper's.

Fifteen minutes before the end of school,
Piper raises his hand.
"Miss Purrypot, can I be excused?"
"In your case, yes," answers the teacher.
"And I hope you will feel better tomorrow."

Piper runs down to a flower shop four blocks away.
"I want some of these yellow roses,"
points out Piper as he puts all his change on the counter.
He gets back in time to catch the bus,
his roses safely concealed under his coat.

At home Piper finds his mother busy
scaling sardines at the kitchen table.
"Hello, Piper," she volunteers
with an attempt at a smile.
"Hello," replies Piper.
He pulls out the bouquet
and lays it down on the table,
in front of his mother.

"Oh, how lovely," she exclaims.

"What a surprise. Are they for me?"

"Yes, if you don't kiss me thank-you," says Piper.

"If you insist, I'll try," promises Mother Paw, smiling.

"Please do," says Piper, smiling back.

NO KISS FOR SON.

NO KISS FOR MOTHER.